To all the girls who have voices that need
to be heard: be bold, be brave, and
raise your hand!—APT

To all the girls, big or small, never forget to
raise your hand and use your voice—MK

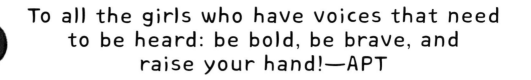

PENGUIN WORKSHOP

An Imprint of Penguin Random House LLC, New York

Penguin supports copyright. Copyright fuels creativity, encourages diverse voices, promotes free speech, and creates a vibrant culture. Thank you for buying an authorized edition of this book and for complying with copyright laws by not reproducing, scanning, or distributing any part of it in any form without permission. You are supporting writers and allowing Penguin to continue to publish books for every reader.

Visit us online at www.penguinrandomhouse.com.

Edited by Renee Hooker
Designed by Julia Rosenfeld

Library of Congress Cataloging-in-Publication Data is available upon request.

ISBN 9781524791209   10 9 8 7 6 5 4 3 2 1

RAISE YOUR HAND

by Alice Paul Tapper

illustrated by Marta Kissi

Penguin Workshop

My name is Alice Paul Tapper, but you can call me Alice.

Mom, Dad + Me ♡

Alice Paul

My mom and dad named me after Alice Paul, a brave woman who fought for women's rights over one hundred years ago.

I'm a **Girl Scout**. I like to have fun and try new things with my troop. One time we earned a horseback riding badge after an afternoon at the stables.

Another time we went into the woods and studied birds, helping us earn our animal habitats badge!

But there have been times when I was afraid
to try things—even things that seemed simple.
I was nervous when we went canoeing.

And I was *really* nervous when I had to go down the zip line on a ropes course!

At school, I get to sit next to my best friends, Joelle and Lucy. I love school, but sometimes it can be scary. "Good morning, class," my teacher said one day. "Who can tell me what the world's largest ocean is?"

My hand shot up.
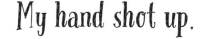
"The Atlantic," I answered.
"I'm sorry, Alice, that's incorrect," she said.
"It's actually the Pacific."

When I realized I got it
wrong, my face felt hot
and my heart thumped
hard in my chest. I tried
not to look at anyone as
I sank lower in my seat.

"Let's try a computer question," my teacher announced. "What do you call an error in a computer program?" *A bug!* I thought, starting to raise my hand. But I wasn't totally sure. And I had already gotten one answer wrong.

I quickly put my hand down. I looked around and realized that only boys had their hands up.

"A virus?" one boy said.

"No, but good try," my teacher told him. "Anyone else?"

I looked at my lap.

"I think it's called a bug," another boy said.

"That's right!" my teacher told him.

I knew it! I thought.

I was still thinking about what had happened when my mom drove me home from school that day. "Mom, are you ever too scared to say something because you might be wrong?" I asked. "Of course," she said. "But I try to be brave and say it anyway. Are you sometimes scared?"

"Yes," I admitted. "And today I noticed that other girls in my class might be, too. But most of the boys aren't. I wish there was something I could do about it."

"Why don't you talk to your Girl Scout troop?" my mom suggested. "Maybe you can come up with something together."

At our next Girl Scout meeting, it turned out I was right about the other girls being nervous.

"I also noticed that the boys were raising their hands more than the girls," Lucy said.
"And once, not one girl raised her hand the whole day!" Harriett added.

"I want to raise my hand, but sometimes it's too scary," Sonia confessed.

"What are you afraid of?" our troop leader asked.

"If I don't get the answer right, people might laugh at me," Sonia said. My friends and I all nodded.

That's when I had an idea.

"We earn patches for doing activities like camping or community service," I said to the others. "What if there was a patch to help girls like us feel more confident in class?"

My friends loved it.
They thought it was
the perfect plan!

My heart thumped
hard in my chest
like it did during
class, but this time
I was smiling.

After that, I got to meet with the Girl Scouts council to talk about my idea. I was nervous but also excited.

They thought it was the best idea they'd heard in a long time! Together, we came up with the Raise Your Hand pledge and patch program.

Everyone we told liked the idea. I even got to talk about it on TV! But I was so scared during the interview, I almost couldn't say anything at all.

It was a lot scarier than raising my hand! But I guess that's part of what made me brave. I was afraid, but I did it anyway.

Some kids at school didn't understand
why we were doing the project.
"You're saying girls are better than
boys," one boy said to me at recess.

But I did not think girls were better than boys. I just wanted girls to believe in themselves.

When I got home from school, my mom had a surprise. "Look, Alice!" she said, showing me the computer screen. "These are messages from Girl Scout troops across the country."

I jumped up and down in excitement. "They're *all* asking to get patches and take the pledge?" I asked. I was amazed that so many girls wanted to be part of the program.

In class the next day, I knew it was time to step up and take the challenge.

So I raised my hand *once* . . .

I didn't always give the right answer. But it wasn't the end of the world. I knew that getting the answer wrong wasn't embarrassing, and speaking up didn't have to be scary.

And I was proud of myself for trying.

So now it's your turn. You can do it.
Be bold, be brave, and

RAISE YOUR
HAND!